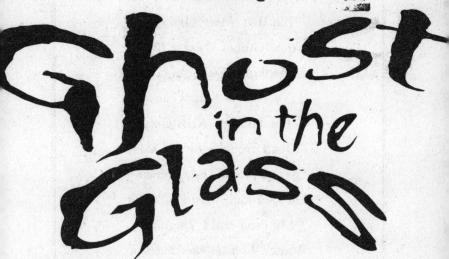

Ghost in the Glass

If you enjoyed reading this book, you might
also like to try another story from the
MAMMOTH READ series:

The Boy Who Swallowed a Ghost *Vivien Alcock*

Big Ben *Rachel Anderson*

Name Games *Theresa Breslin*

Shadowflight *Franzeska G Ewart*

£10,000 *Keith Gray*

The Runner *Keith Gray*

Dead Trouble *Keith Gray*

Secret Friend *Pete Johnson*

The Gargoyle *Garry Kilworth*

My Frog and I *Jan Mark*

Winter Wolf *Lynne Markham*

Is That Your Dog? *Steve May*

Little Dad *Pat Moon*

Tommy Trouble *Stephen Potts*

Hurricane Summer *Robert Swindells*

Roger's War *Robert Swindells*

Doodlebug Alley *Robert Swindells*

Size Twelve *Robert Westall*

Ghost in the Glass

Caroline Pitcher

illustrated by Karin Littlewood

Mammoth

To Celia Frank, who makes beautiful stained glass
C.P.

For Karen
K.L.

First published in Great Britain in 2001
by Mammoth, an imprint of Egmont Books UK
a division of Egmont Holding Limited
239 Kensington High Street, London W8 6SA

Text copyright © 2001 Caroline Pitcher
Illustrations copyright © 2001 Karin Littlewood

The moral rights of the author and illustrator have been asserted

ISBN 0 7497 4448 0

1 3 5 7 9 10 8 6 4 2

Printed in Great Britain
by Cox & Wyman Ltd, Reading, Berkshire

Contents

~

1. Silver

In the window stands a woman with a dress of
  ruby red.
Her skin is white as china.
Her eyes are green as watercress in a clear, fast
  stream.
Take care . . .

'I don't *want* to go home!' cried Christina.
'All we've looked at in this stupid museum is

old toys and rocks!'

Her mother sighed. 'Great Aunt May is tired now. We must get her home.'

Christina looked down at the old lady in the wheelchair. Great Aunt May's eyes were closed.

'It's cos she's never asleep at night!' cried Grace, Christina's little sister. 'She sits up with her eyes wide open. She watches the window. *All* night long.'

'How do you know, Grace?' called their father.

There was no reply. Grace went skipping off round a case of Roman jewellery, singing loudly with her hands over her ears.

Christina said, 'Grace knows because she sneaks downstairs in the middle of the night and eats whole packets of Golden Crunchies *and* never gets told off!'

'Don't tell tales, Christina,' snapped Dad.

Grace danced back to them. She wailed, 'I want to go home too!'

'Well I don't.'

Dad said, 'Come on, Chris. Be reasonable. It's a family outing.'

'Don't call me Chris,' she snarled, thinking, *the family is* me *too. Why do they always gang up against me, in favour of Grace? We had to come here just because she's doing Victorian toys at school. Look at her, dabbing her fist at her eye and sniffing. And not a tear in sight*! Sometimes Christina wanted to hit Grace, *hard*, so the best thing to do was go. She turned on her heel and fled away from them through the galleries, watched by small bronze gods and buddhas. She stormed up a marble staircase.

They won't get the wheelchair up here in a hurry!

In a corner a suit of armour slumped

against the wall.

I could get into that and clank through the rooms with pointy metal feet. I'd have one of those spiked things like an iron conker case and swing it round my head, CRASH BANG SMASH! The thought made her smile and slow down.

Dim shapes hung on the walls around her, treacle-dark portraits of people who did not want to be in their frames. Christina saw a sad-faced woman in a dark satin dress, three small boys uncomfortable in sailor suits with snow-white collars, and a marshmallow-faced woman nursing a powder-puff dog. How did she keep it *still* long enough to be painted?

Maybe I can persuade them to go to a cafe, thought Christina? *Grace will be easy. Just say jam doughnuts. I don't want to go back home. I don't like home today.*

It was something to do with Great Aunt

May. Now they were in the new house, Mum and Dad felt they could have her to stay for a few days because she could sleep downstairs. They had put a bed for her in the study.

Christina felt two things about Great Aunt May. One, she was a dear little old lady with silver hair who never said a word. Two, something restless had come to the house with her. It made Christina uneasy.

A beautiful horse of blue-green stone reared up from a stand. Christina glanced over her shoulder. At the other end of the gallery, the museum attendant sat motionless on his chair. She reached out her hand and stroked the horse, admiring his flaring nostrils and wild mane.

An icy finger-tip touched the back of her neck. Someone was watching her. She looked around.

It was a woman, taller than life.

High on the wall she stood, dazzling Christina with her beauty. She wore a dress of ruby red. Her face was white as bone china, and her hair of amber-gold flowed down past her shoulders. She was gazing into the distance, searching for something far away with eyes as green as emeralds.

'Those colours!' whispered Christina. 'They're the colours of jewels!'

This woman wasn't painted in treacle. She was made out of stained glass, with sky behind her of brilliant blue. The bright grass at her feet was starred with white flowers. The huge piece of glass was shaped like a continent on a map, as if some parts of it were missing.

A glass jigsaw . . . I wonder who she is? Stained glass is usually for churches, but she's certainly not a saint, or an angel.

Suddenly the museum attendant blew his nose like a trombone. Perhaps he was used to people thinking he was a model and wanted to show that he was real?

He turned his head towards Christina and called, 'She's a colourful lady, isn't she? It's her self-portrait in glass. See that drawing next to her? It's her plan for the whole window, but there's only her left.'

In the drawing, three birds fluttered around the woman. One had just alighted on the woman's finger and was folding its wings. On her left side stood someone else. It was a pencil outline, no face, no details. Just a small faint shape.

'What happened to the rest of the window?' asked Christina. 'Didn't she make it?'

'Yes, but it got smashed,' he said. 'She's all that survived.'

Christina winced. 'How terrible to break something so beautiful. Who did it?'

The attendant shrugged. 'Dunno,' he said. 'Vandals. Or enemies, maybe. Sounds like she was a very strange woman.'

He rustled his paper. He'd had enough of talking. Shame, because Christina wanted to hear more about the woman. She also wanted an ice-cream soda, but as she walked out of the gallery she glanced back.

The glass woman's eyes had moved. She was watching Christina.

They always say that about pictures, don't they? The Mona Lisa is supposed to look back at you, and the eyes of that hairy Cavalier in the big hat follow you round the room.

The glass woman wanted something. She was just about to step down from the wall!

Suddenly Christina wanted to be with her family. She ran back down the marble staircase.

It didn't take long to fall out with them again . . .

'No, we *can't* go to a cafe, Christina,' hissed her father. 'May is all agitated. I don't think she likes it here.'

Christina glanced at her great aunt and saw that it was true. Great Aunt May's hands were twisting and turning and her pale face was tight with fear.

Something about the museum terrified her.

2. China white

It was still dark when Christina woke.

She hadn't slept well. She'd had odd dreams. There were angry shouts and sounds of breaking glass, yet the dream was so blurred she couldn't see what was happening.

Monday. She took a while to put up her hair. Lately she had fancied wearing it drawn up on top of her head, like a ballerina, but it kept slipping down. No-one had commented (except Alastair in 9B who had said, 'Eugh! Pinhead!') but Christina thought it made her look older. She hated going down to the kitchen before school. You might have to talk to people, people such as your mum as she edged her way around the table in a limp blue dressing-gown, with washing for the machine and orange juice for Grace. Or your father, slowly stirring his porridge as he gazed at the wall. Or, worst of all, your wretched little sister. Grace stood at the table, delving deep into a pot of chocolate spread with a big spoon.

'You didn't get any more cereal, Mum,' said Christina, shaking the last few golden circles out of the box. She sloshed on milk and the few pieces rose to the surface. She picked up the bowl and drank it straight.

'Don't be disgusting, Christina,' snapped

Mum. 'And I can't go shopping every single day.'

On the table lay the guide-book from the museum. Christina turned the pages carefully, then caught her breath. There she was! That china-white face stared up at Christina.

'Who's that?' cried Grace, snatching at the book, but Christina growled, 'Geddoff!' and turned away with it held high so that Grace couldn't see.

'Stop it, you two!' groaned Dad.

Grace pouted and went back to the chocolate spread. Christina looked at the tall woman in the photograph. Fancy draining all those jewelled colours into a black and white photograph.

Woman in North Window it said underneath in squiggly writing, and continued:

Floriane Mortelle was a minor artist who often worked in stained glass. Her finest work was a self-portrait in the great North Window of her house in Dolmen Way. In her day, Floriane Mortelle's name was linked with scandal. It was said that she possessed magic powers. Some said she was a sorceress.

Stop reading, warned a little voice in Christina's head. She ignored it, and read, 'The local painter, Orlando Dunne, accused her of witchcraft.'

'Christina,' called Mum. 'Here, take your auntie a cup of tea. I've got her all washed and dressed. I hope you're going to be a bit nicer to her today. Nicer to us *all*, please!'

'I just wish she would *say* something,' insisted Christina. 'She's like a mute. It makes me feel odd having her in the house when she never speaks.'

15

'Don't be so selfish.'

'She's not my real aunt anyway,' snapped Christina.

'She's Dad's Great Aunt by marriage,' said Mum, 'and it shouldn't matter *who* she is. Just be nice to her. It's good to have her to stay for a few days, isn't it?'

'I didn't say it wasn't, did I? I just said she makes me feel odd.'

'Why does Auntie May have that baby's cup?' piped up Grace, pointing at the plastic drinker.

'Why do you have chocolate spread all over your face?' sneered Christina.

She took the drinker into the living room. Great Aunt May lolled in the high-backed chair as if she was a rag doll. Mum had wedged her in with cushions.

Christina looked down at May's small face. Her skin was like that rice paper Mum had bought when she made macaroons. May's shoulders were frail as birds' wings in a cardigan of palest pink. Why was she always dressed in baby colours? Why not a nice turquoise or purple to brighten her up?

Christina knelt down by the chair and took the old lady's hands, one at a time, and closed them gently round the cup. She saw

that the hands were criss-crossed with thin white scars. She whispered, 'Sorry I dashed off in the museum yesterday, Great Aunt May. I wanted to see upstairs. You didn't miss much. Just some dusty old paintings and some stained glass.'

May turned slowly towards her. Christina looked into her eyes and was shocked. They were so full of feeling.

Back in the kitchen she grabbed the chocolate spread from Grace.

'You've got it all over you!' she said viciously.

Grace pulled her fingers through her long fair hair and sucked them free of chocolate. She said, 'I don't know why we have to have old Auntie here. She stares at me. She's good for a cuddle, though.'

Dad laughed. 'I'm glad you cuddle her, Grace! But don't be rough. May had a bad stroke years ago. She's never spoken since. She's fragile, you know.'

'She didn't last into her nineties by being fragile,' said Mum. 'Something has kept her going.'

Christina remembered May's eyes and silently agreed. She asked, 'Why has Great Aunt May got all those scars on her hands, Dad?'

He shrugged. 'Gardening? Rose thorns? I dunno. Now Christina, you'll have to walk to school. I'm leaving later than usual this morning.'

He's still cross with me from the museum, she thought. Good, I like the walk to school on my own. For a short time I'm not part of a family and not part of a tutor group.

Her mum was chuntering on, 'Too much to do this week. And May staying. And I can't pick you up from school on Thursday,

Christina, because I've got to take Grace to the dentist.'

Fine, just fine! Christina ran upstairs to pull her PE kit from under her bed, stuffed it into her bag, wishing too late she had put it out to wash.

As she ran back down, she suddenly remembered the glass woman staring at her. A flicker of fear moved in her stomach.

3. Iron black

The sky was as dim and grey as pigeon's feathers.

Christina wandered along to school, then stopped. An ice puddle filled a dip in the pavement. She couldn't resist it. One foot stamped in the middle, and cracks ran out across the surface with a satisfying CRUNCH as if it was clear glass.

She glanced up.

She had never noticed these gates before,

although she must pass them whenever she walked to school. They were made of thick black iron, wrought with lilies and leaves and twisting stems, making her think of the thorn hedge that grew up around Sleeping Beauty's castle. This morning the iron was silvered with cold. The gates were fastened by a heavy padlock. Christina stared through them, down the winding drive, at the house of sombre red brick.

Looks like some spooky temple. I wouldn't fancy living there, she thought and walked on, past the new estate, round the corner, into the newsagents for some mints, past the flower stall and on to school.

Halfway through maths, Christina remembered that the dark red house was in Dolmen Way, where the glass woman had lived.

Christina was always starving when she came in from school. Every day she ate at least two slices of thickly-buttered bread, and every day her mother sighed, 'You won't eat your supper.' Christina did, if it was something she liked, and didn't if it had anything green in it. Tonight she saw Mum constructing a pie with puff pastry, so that was all right.

Great Aunt May sat at the table. She wore the shawl Christina's mum had made her. It was a web of soft blue wool. By her hand was a notebook and a pencil. Sometimes May could write down what she wanted instead of having to struggle for words.

Grace sat opposite her, dressing her dolls. *Sweet as candy*, thought Christina sourly. Great Aunt May was watching with her head on one side like a bird. *Watching Grace, not me. Watching her like everyone does because she's pretty, with her long fair hair and blue, blue eyes. But May stares so intently at her! She's fascinated by Grace. Why? And . . .*

Thoughts darted through Christina's head like birds. She shook her head to be free of them and said, 'Would you like some of this lovely fresh bread, Aunt May? I'll cut it paper-thin.'

May inclined her head. *Great*, thought Christina, *permission to pig out*.

'My doll needs more clothes,' announced Grace and disappeared upstairs.

Christina cut May's bread into four neat triangles. While she was buttering the bread she asked, 'Mum? Do you know anything about the big houses in Dolmen Way?'

Great Aunt May was watching *her* now, and listening, her head to one side.

'There were grand houses there years ago,' said Mum. 'They were made into flats. I used to wheel you past there in your buggy.'

'What, B.G.?'

Her mum laughed. 'Yes. *Long* Before Grace. Seven years before Grace. When you used to tell me how much you wanted a little sister.'

'I can't believe *that*!' said Christina.

'Yes you did. And you loved her. I remembered that I couldn't stand *my* little brother at first.'

'But you and Uncle John are big buddies.'

'We are *now*,' smiled her mum, 'and so will you and Grace be one day soon.'

I'm not picking up that *talking stick*, thought Christina crossly.

Mum scored the pastry top with her knife and said, 'I thought all those big houses in Dolmen Way had been demolished.'

'No. There's one left,' said Christina. 'It's got towers and turrets and an overgrown garden. It's a sort of *Psycho* house. Some artist woman used to live there. I saw . . .'

she took a deep breath, 'I saw her in a stained glass window at the museum.'

'So that's where you ran off to,' said Mum, opening up the oven so that heat rushed out. 'That's what all this house stuff is about. I wish you wouldn't be so secretive, Christina. I wish you'd tell us things.'

'Why should you be interested anyway?'

Mum put the pie on the top shelf and closed up the oven. 'I think I'll go and wash my hair,' she sighed.

Christina prepared the bread and butter. Just a thin sheen of jam on May's bread, seedless bramble jelly. Thick strawberry with great fruity lumps on her own. She chose a pretty china plate with roses round the edge for May. Why should she always have to have plastic things? She set the plate down in front of May and said, 'Here you are, Auntie!'

Her smile died away as she saw that the old lady was trembling. *She's frightened of something again.*

Grace bounced back and tugged Christina's sleeve. 'Where's that booklet with that big woman?' she wittered.

'Shut up and go away,' hissed Christina. She heard the whoosh of the kitchen door and Grace's feet clatter on the stairs as she rushed off to tell Mum about her horrible big sister.

Christina knelt down so that she could feel the faint quick breaths as May struggled for words, and could not find them. 'What is it, Great Aunt May?' she whispered. Some sound was there, like seals, or eels . . . wild steel? Christina could not make sense of it.

She handed Great Aunt May the pencil. It fell onto the floor. Christina picked it up and closed May's fingers on it again. She saw May take a deep breath and control her trembling. Head bent, she seemed to be writing. It took ages.

At last May let the pencil drop and Christina picked up the pad. On the top sheet she could just see May's writing, as faint as if a spider had picked its way across the paper with little feet of lead: handkerchiefs . . . talc . . .

And lower down the page, darker than the other messages, pressed deep into the pad: *child stealer*.

Aunt May's eyes flew open wide. Her eyes searched Christina's face.

Christina reached for May's trembling hand and cupped it in her own.

4. Eel green

The words *child stealer* tumbled through Christina's mind. If *only* May could talk. Christina couldn't stop thinking about it, so when she took the bread and bramble jelly the next day, she asked, 'Auntie . . . did you ever know a woman who made stained glass windows?'

Crash! The pretty plate dropped out of May's hands onto the floor. It lay there in two white wings. The old lady's eyes stared at something Christina could not see.

'What on earth . . . Leave her alone, Christina!' cried Mum, fussing up to them. 'You're too much for her! And what were you doing giving her bone china?'

'Why shouldn't she have it!' cried Christina, storming out of the room. Never mind. She could wait until Thursday, when Mum wasn't collecting her after school, and she could find out more.

Thursday came.

Christina was tired, and her head felt bruised with dreams. Someone had been following her in the dreams, but Christina could not − or would not − see the face.

The day seemed to last for ever.

She realised too late that she had forgotten her English homework and she was told off for yawning in double science.

The only lesson she looked forward to, history, was an anti-climax because Mr Watkins had got flu, and the supply teacher was no match for the clowns in the form. She shivered in the corner of the hockey field, hoping they would all forget about her, and spent as long as she possibly could finding the ball from round the back of the pavilion.

The moment lessons were over, she hurried off along the road, via the newsagent's to stock up on mints. Her tummy felt odd, as if something was wriggling in it, and she told herself mints helped. There was no flower seller today. She must have given up in the cold.

She walked on round the corner, and then stopped.

At the roadside was a builder's skip. It was filled with rubble, like an orange ark. The thorn-hedge gates stood wide open.

Christina tiptoed across the pavement, not quite daring to put her foot past the gate.

The drive wound its way through a shrubbery of laurel bushes, their glossy leaves as spotted with yellow as salamander skins. Christina glanced back, but she knew she was going through those gates. She had known for days.

The house must have been grand in its day, but now it was almost a ruin. She saw a flash of yellow. It was a truck with huge caterpillar tracks, loaded with a small crane.

At the front of the house was a stone porch with the windows knocked out, empty as an old bus shelter. The door had a brass knocker. It was a head, but it was covered with green mould so that you couldn't see its face. Its hair was a like tangle of green eels.

I'm not touching that! There's no-one to answer

it anyway. Is there?

She stared up at the turreted front of the house. It was like a stage set, a façade. Much of the house had fallen down, or been destroyed.

'I'll just have a look round the back,' she told herself. She knew she was trespassing, and had already planned what to say if she met someone. She'd tell them she was studying old houses for school. Yet still her heart was thumping as if it was up inside her head.

Down the side was a passageway. Small ferns and pincushions of moss grew from hidden pockets in the wall. Christina saw islands of amber lichen and almost trod on a snail. Streaks of something dark glistened on the brick.

At the end of the passageway was a low door, just open.

Eugh! The smell! Christina was used to the smell of her new house, paint and fresh plaster, polish and varnished wood. This house smelled damp and sickly, like blue cheese, and she took a deep breath before giving the door a little push.

There was a kitchen with cooking ranges, tall cupboards built into the wall, and a stone sink. She tiptoed into a wide hallway. The floor of the hall was a mosaic of coloured stones, making flowers and leaves. There were birds with blue wings. She was walking on a garden. What was that? Footsteps behind her? She looked over her shoulder. No-one was there.

'Don't be stupid, Christina,' she said out loud.

She tiptoed up some stone steps, and stopped, astonished.

The room was vast. High above, the

ceiling was split by beams.

It's like being inside a ribcage.

In a corner stood a Chinese vase of peacock feathers with their green eyes filmed by dust. The walls were hung thickly with brocade and torn tapestries. The hangings swarmed with winged creatures, griffins and serpents, a dragon with ragged wings trailing spokes like a worn umbrella, and birds with hooked beaks.

She reached out her hand to touch the hangings but snatched it back at once. It came away sticky, as if she had plunged it into a spider's web.

At the far side of the room a great staircase swept up out of sight. She took a step to cross towards it and something crunched beneath her foot. Glass. Broken glass. For once Christina was glad to be wearing her clumpy school shoes.

Along the wall lay crumpled shapes of
iron. They were old cages. For parrots, or

budgies? She picked her way across to the staircase, touched the banister and found it furred with dust. She craned her neck to see to the top. It was light up there. The roof was open to the sky as if it had been lifted off by a giant hand.

The hugeness of it all made Christina think she was in some kind of place of worship.

And then she saw the faces.

All the way up the wall by the stairs there were faces, grinning down at her.

They were masks, *hideous* masks. Some had beaks, some had scales and long teeth, even horns. At one time they had been painted. She could see flakes of red and black. Who would want to live with them?

The north end of the room was light. There was a great hole in the wall.

So that's *where the woman's window had been!*

39

How did it get smashed?

Christina felt uneasy, as if there was something in the room with her. She listened. The room was breathing.

She stood quite still, sensing tiny points of colour swirling and gathering, as if the glass woman with the emerald eyes was growing and taking shape, ready to tower over her.

'No!' shouted Christina.

She ran out of the room and into the kitchen, just as the great metal ball swung into the wall and the house fell down all around her.

5. Ruby red

Dust. Dust swirling, making her cough.

In the darkness a voice cried, *Let me out!*
Please, let me out of here!

Christina struggled to sit up. She couldn't
feel broken bones, but she was bruised from
her fall, and shaking with shock. She
searched for a tissue and blinked away dust
and tears.

The kitchen wall was gone. Bricks lay
everywhere. She could see the yellow crane

with its breaker ball hanging still on the chain now. The driver leaned against the cab, chatting to another man in a hard hat. They didn't even know she was there.

It could have killed me.

She sneezed and blew her nose. The dust cleared slowly. Christina could hardly breathe.

She stared across the kitchen. The battering had damaged the sink so that a zigzag crack ran down the side. The fireplace was at an angle now, and one of the little doors to the black range ovens hung open. Inside, something gleamed in the darkness. Christina knew she should get out – suppose it happened again? Instead, she was drawn to the range. She struggled to her feet and limped across the kitchen.

She put her hand into the oven, groping until her hand closed round a soft bundle.

The fabric had almost disintegrated. Gently she turned it back.

It was full of glass, three birds of glass. They were dark blue with a blush of red. Two had wings curved in flight. The third was folding its wings, ready to alight.

'Swallows,' she whispered.

They were beautiful. But what were they doing hidden in the range? It was as if they had been buried alive.

Each bird had graceful tail streamers and a fixed yellow eye. Some wing-tips were chipped, and cracks ran across the deep blue. One bird's beak was blunted.

She heard a shout from the workmen. Time to go. She tucked the glass birds inside her schoolbag, noticing for the first time the blood trickling from her fingers. *Red as rubies*, she thought foolishly.

Head down, she ran through the remains of the passageway and along the drive. Behind her she heard the *BOOM* of the demolition ball as it hit the house again.

She hurried home. With luck, Great Aunt May would be propped up in her chair and Christina could show her the swallows while

Mum was out. She felt sure the birds should have been in Floriane's window. So why weren't they?

More and more, Christina felt that Floriane and May were set together in the same strange story. Would May ever be able to speak to her about it?

But when she got home, there was a note from Mum:

CHRISTINA, MAY'S IN BED. SHE'S NOT WELL. PLEASE BE V. QUIET. LUV MUM

Christina washed the blood carefully from her hands and thought, *if May's not well, I can't start asking her about Floriane Mortelle and her window. I just can't.*

She propped the birds against her bedroom wall. When she heard the front door open, she put her art folder in front to hide them. This was *her* secret.

6. Enamel blue

Floriane walks through her house of shadows, her satin skirts swishing on the stone floor. She looks down at her hands. Such short, strong hands she has! Hands that can hack and cut and piece together windows and screens. Such rough skin, such torn, ragged fingernails, stained black with the lead she uses to fit her glass mosaics of astounding colour together.

The masks on the wall watch in horror as Floriane walks on and into Christina's dreams.

Deep in her sleep, Christina hears the twittering of birds.

She watches the swallows swoop and soar, slender crescents of enamel blue and red, with

49

tapering tail streamers and tiny heads. Their wings brush her face. It feels more like a graze. They scratch at her with glass beaks and claws. They fly at her window as if they would dash themselves to pieces.

Something begins to shape itself on the other side. A cloud of red forms and gathers together and two points of green light glitter. They'll set the curtain on fire!

'No!' cries Christina, 'No!'

She sat up in bed and fumbled for the light-switch.

Her eyes wouldn't open properly.

Her head hurt. She had been buffeted about on a rough sea of dreams.

For the last few days someone had been stalking her, in her dreams and in her waking hours. Now she knew who it was. Someone with eyes of emerald green.

'Floriane!' she told herself. 'It's Floriane and her birds!'

She looked across to the wall where she had propped the birds before she'd gone to sleep. They hadn't moved at all. But they had been trying to get out! And *she* was trying . . . Christina daren't put it into words in case she saw it happen right in front of her. She put them behind her art folder.

She slid out of bed and tiptoed over to the window.

Don't draw back the curtain. Wait. Make sure.

Christina twitched the curtain and peeped out onto just another gloomy February morning. Light was struggling to find its way into the day.

A robin strutted on the fence. Another robin landed near him. They faced each other like tiny fighting cocks, twig legs stretched out in fury. All they saw in the

51

world were rival robins. *So that was the twittering*, thought Christina with relief.

There was no-one on the street that she could see, no lights, nothing. Why should there be? It was just a nightmare.

When she was small, Christina had nightmares about a horse, again and again. She knew it wasn't real. It was a painted rocking horse from a roundabout, dappled with yellow spots. The horse had long teeth and staring eyes. In her dreams it chased her with a funny rocking run and she would wake up sick with fright and look round her bedroom for tell-tale hoofprints. She knew it didn't have real hooves, but that didn't help.

So she made up a wild horse in her head. He was midnight black, with a strong arched neck crested with a thick mane. His nostrils flared, lined with scarlet, as he reared up before the spotted horse on his powerful haunches and raked the air with his devil's hooves, then crashed down in a shower of bright sparks.

The spotted roundabout horse turned and rocked away down the stairs and out of the house. It did not come back.

Now, Christina thought, *I could do with a wild horse to chase this woman away*.

Friday. Her fright at the old house, and her bad dreams, had left Christina feeling drained. Once again, the day passed by just out of her reach.

When she got home she sank down at the table. Mum was washing potatoes.

Great Aunt May was a little better. She sat in the lounge staring out through the french windows. Christina hesitated a moment, then kissed her gently on her paper-white forehead. Their eyes met and May smiled.

She's so frail and weak. Yet I look into her eyes and see strength, and passion.

The door banged.

Grace ran into the room shrieking, with a friend close on her heels. Grace wore her new shiny red shoes and she loved to dance and stamp in them. Sweet little Grace must be the loudest child in the world! Grace by name and not by nature. The two girls tore out of the room and up the stairs.

'What a row!' grumbled Christina. 'Why does she always have to be shouting and charging all over the house, Mum? I thought May was supposed to be kept quiet? So why does Grace always have friends round?'

'Grace is not as private as you are, darling. She likes company all the time. Sounds to me as if the green-eyed monster is talking!'

'There's no green-eyed monster!' shouted Christina. 'Grace gets everything! All the fuss, all the looking-after.'

'I'm sorry if it seems that way, Christina. I don't think you're right. She does get more looking-after, as you call it, because she is seven years younger than you are. After all, you had seven years of all the attention before she was even born.'

'Oh *really*! You *always* protect her, always.'

'Just as we protected you when you were small. And we still do. When you'll let us, that is! Grace really admires you. She looks up to you, Chris.'

'Don't call me Chris!' she snapped and turned away from her mother's outstretched hand.

The door flew open. Grace hurtled in. 'Biscuits, please!' she shrieked.

As Mum shook out biscuits onto a plate, Grace stared at Christina. 'Your hair looks lovely, Christina,' she said. 'Looks like a nice big doughnut.'

'Hmm . . .' murmured Christina. Her face grew pink with Grace's compliment. She thought of giving Grace one of her packets of mints. *No*.

She went into her bedroom and shut the door. She could still hear them squealing. She took off her coat, opened a book and tried to start her homework, but she couldn't concentrate. She moved the folder so that she could see the glass birds. They were just as she had left them, quite still. Yet Christina felt drawn to look at them again and again.

'You're very beautiful, you three,' she told them. 'I saw you in her sketch for the window. You belong in the window. Why were you shut up in the oven?'

There was a loud knock and the door handle turned.

'Mum says You-must-make-May's-bread-and-butter, Christina. Ooh!' she cried as her eyes lit on the glass birds. 'Are they real?'

'Of course they're not, silly,' said Christina.

'I don't like them. They're too gleamy and hard. They should go in a window. That's where they live, I think.'

'Maybe,' said Christina grudgingly.

'They're like boomerangs,' cried Grace. 'Boomerang birds!'

Grace is right. Their wings are curved into a boomerang shape.

In the kitchen Christina prepared May's tea.

Great Aunt May was staring through the french windows into the dark garden. When

Christina touched her arm, the old lady's lips twitched in a small smile. Her eyes came to life for a second. Then the spark was switched off. It was like watching a dot fade from the screen of a TV set.

'Shall I close the curtains for you?' asked Christina, but May shook her head and turned back to watch the darkness.

The pad of paper lay on the table. Christina edged it towards her. They were still there. The words, *child stealer*.

Underneath, May had written something else:

Take care.

Floriane Mortelle. The Sorceress. She *was the child stealer*!

Christina knew that now. She knew from her fear in the museum, in the house in Dolmen Way. Who did she steal?

How did May know about it?

Too bad, Floriane! thought Christina, *because now you're just made of glass and you've no powers left!*

If only she could be sure about that.

7. Emerald

Christina struggled to wake up, but couldn't. It wasn't really *her* in the dream. It was someone smaller.

The room is cold and sickly-sweet with incense.

The tall lady wants to sketch me. She says she wants to draw my long fair hair and my lovely blue dress with the white collar. She lays a sheaf of white lilies along my arm.

'Stand very still, my dear,' she says sternly.

61

Ooh! What's that in those cages in the shadows? Birds! Small birds that hop and flutter and sing their tiny songs. Pretty canaries and larks.

'I love my birds more than anything,' says the tall lady. 'That's why I lock them up. They must stay with me always.'

Yes, she loves her prisoner birds. And her coloured glass. That's all she loves. And she is angry with my father, because he loves Mama best and his pictures are better than hers. Everybody says so!

On the floor there are some shiny birds. Swallows. I want to see them fly, so I cup them in my hands and I throw them up into the air, so blue and pretty!

Oh . . .

I hear her scream with rage. 'Why didn't you do as you were told!' and I put up my hands to cover my eyes, and I spread my fingers and peep through, and . . . the tall lady is walking towards me!

Her voice is low and cold. 'What have you done, child? The birds were for my portrait.' She points at the great north window. I see the lady again in the window, all blurry through my tears. She's made of stained glass. Behind the lady is such a blue blue sky, blue as those flowers Mama told me not to touch. 'Monkshood flowers are poisonous,' says Mama.

The glass lady has a pearly skin and golden hair. She is beautiful.

But the lady down here in the room is ugly! Her hair is carroty-orange. Her face is hard as a flat-iron. Her eyes are horrid, green as the stones on a grave. She has stubby hands, all scratchy from cutting up her glass.

Father says this lady makes spells. He says she's bad. Why did I let her bring me here? Father doesn't know where I am!

And there's someone behind that window.

There's a shadow, as if someone is spying. The tall lady wraps the broken birds in soft pink chenille.

'I will hide my poor birds to keep them safe,' she says. 'That is what you do to keep things. You shut them up where no-one can find them.'

Oh!

I listen to her long skirts swish as she walks out of the room. When the swishing stops I run across the room and down the garden in the hall and hurl myself at the front door, but it will not open, so back down to the kitchens and the dark passage and to the other door, and that's locked too, so I scream, 'Papa! Mama! Let me out of here!'

Christina surfaced at last from her dreams. She felt sick and bewildered. One thing she knew: the birds should not be here in her house. They should not be with her family. The museum was the right place for them. Someone should put them back.

Christina skipped breakfast and packed the birds carefully in her bag.

'I'm going to have another look in the museum, Mum,' she said.

'That's a good idea, love! Why don't you take Grace with you?'

'No! I want to go on my own.'

'Oh *please* take Grace. She loved it last time.'

'No she didn't! She wanted to go home! She pretended to cry.'

'Yes, but that was late on a Sunday when she'd stayed up the night before, and she was tired. Go on! Grace would love to spend some time with you.'

'Oh *yeah*,' sneered Christina, but some of her anger ebbed away in spite of herself. She remembered Grace saying the swallows should go home to their window, like boomerangs that always return. Maybe

Grace had some part to play in all this.

'Don't go so fast,' cried Grace. 'You're hurting my hand.'

'Sorry,' said Christina, slowing down. She wanted to get the task done and finished.

'Old Auntie didn't like the museum, did she?' said Grace. 'And Auntie's leaving tomorrow, isn't she?'

Of course! Tomorrow was Sunday and they were taking Great Aunt May back to her nursing home. *I'll miss her*, thought Christina with astonishment. *There's something binding us together. I must find out what it is before she goes.*

As they turned the corner they caught the scent of flowers on the cold air and came to the flower stall. Christina glowed at the prospect of doing something right for once.

'I'm going to buy flowers for May,' she

said. 'She can take them back to her room at the home!'

The large sprays were a pound each, and they weren't even what Christina meant by 'flowers'. They were big and showy with heavy heads and she didn't want them. What would Great Aunt May really like?

She saw the freesias, delicate on their slender stems, cream, pale pink and lilac. She leaned over and breathed in their sweet smell. Great Aunt May would love them. After all, what good were flowers without a scent?

'I'll have two lots, please,' she said. 'And some anemones.' The anemones looked as if they were made of crimson and purple-like satin, almost too lovely to be real.

'Christina, look!' cried Grace, pointing to the back of the stall. 'Angels blow those!' She reached towards the tall white lilies.

Christina tried not to laugh. She could see the picture in Grace's mind, of fat little cherubs blowing these flowers like white trumpets.

From the deep middles of the lilies sprang black stamens, furry as spider's legs.

'I want some of them for Mum,' cried Grace.

'Oh Grace, honestly! I haven't enough money for those as well!' said Christina.

'*Well, I've* got enough money,' boasted Grace. 'I've brought my pocket money. So there!' She stuck out her hand to the flower seller. The woman looked at the money and picked out three lilies. She wrapped them in green tissue and laid them in Grace's arms.

'Be careful with them,' warned Christina. The sight of her sister holding those lilies made her feel uneasy.

The museum was almost empty of people.

Christina and Grace hurried past the jewellery and coins, old urns and vases, the bronze gods and fat little buddhas.

'Can we see that big woman?' cried Grace. 'The one in the book?'

'Urm . . . I don't know,' frowned Christina, yet as she was drawn back to that gallery, she pulled Grace with her.

They stood in the doorway. Christina peered in. She saw the gleam of gilded frames and the dust shining in the slanting winter sunlight.

The sunlight had a sharpness that shouted *DANGER!*

Christina saw emerald green in that sharp light, and in the same instant realised that the attendant wasn't there.

'You stay here, Grace,' she said. 'I won't be a second.'

'No!' said Grace. 'I'm coming with you.'

Grace let go of her hand. 'I like spooky old things,' she said and ran into the room.

'Wait!' cried Christina, running after her.

I'm not looking up there. I don't want to see her, she thought, dropping the flowers and scrabbling for the birds in her bag. Points of heat glowed on her back, as if someone was holding up glass to the sun to start a fire.

She heard Grace cry, 'Ooh!'

She stood up and saw her little sister walking as if she was in a trance. Grace's mouth was open, her eyes wide, the white lilies lying along her arm, and Christina was back in her dream!

The sun slanted on the dress of ruby red, spilling like blood onto the floor, and she heard harsh breathing. Christina knew what would happen.

'No Grace, no!' she shouted.

The woman towered above them, holding

out her hand for Grace to join her.

'*Come to me, child!*'

Christina heard her sister whimper, and she drew herself up, willing herself as tall and strong as Floriane, shouting, '*No! You won't have her! You won't!*'

She hurled the birds towards the stained glass woman. '*Take them instead!*' she cried, remembering suddenly her horse of midnight black. She turned and her hand found the stone horse on its plinth.

'*Leave me my sister, Floriane Mortelle!*' cried Christina. '*Take your birds and go! Or I will break you, you Sorceress!*'

The room grew hot. It rippled with molten glass. The world turned and spun on its axis, scattering crimson and emerald, gold and china white, and the purple of anemones. The world roared in her ears, she heard hooves strike, sparks fly, glass crack and shatter.

For a moment, there was nothing. Time stopped.

And then someone grabbed her hand.

'That big lady, Christina! I don't like her!' bawled Grace. 'I nearly got cut to pieces! And Mum's lovely lilies are all broken, look!' Grace kicked the lilies hard so that they spun across the floor. She looked up at Christina and said admiringly, '*You* weren't scared, were you, Chrissie? *You* told her!'

Christina stroked the stone horse, then knelt to pick up her flowers. She said, 'We can get more flowers for Mum, Grace. Different ones. Don't worry,' and she heard her voice shaking.

'Morning!' called the attendant, shuffling back in. 'I've just been on my coffee break. Is this your little sister?'

'Yes. This is Grace,' said Christina.

'And do you like the lovely glass lady,

73

dear?' he asked Grace.

'No. She's horrible!' shouted Grace.

As they left the room, Christina made herself look back.

She saw three swallows in the stained glass window. Two flew around the woman. One had alighted on her hand. They were unbroken, shining blue purple and red as the petals of her anemones.

No more dreams, she thought, exhilarated. Just one mystery left.

8. Gold

Grace skipped down the corridor to the office. When they had collected Great Aunt May she had taken a fancy to Matron's little dog. 'It's like one of those mops on a stick with long bits!' she cried. 'But it's orange.'

'We'll just see Matron, Christina,' said Mum. 'You take May and settle her in.'

'Can she stay with us again?' asked Christina, catching May's shy smile.

'Of course she can!' said Mum. She

looked at Christina in surprise.

Christina pushed the wheelchair along the corridor of the nursing home. She glanced down at Great Aunt May and caught the scent of the freesias. The old lady had been so pleased with her flowers, holding them against her cheek to breathe in the scent.

In the neat little room, Christina eased her Aunt's coat off her shoulders. She slid back the wardrobe door and put the coat on a hanger.

Leaning against a wall at the end there was a package wrapped in corrugated cardboard.

She felt May watching her. 'Can I look, please?' she asked, and May inclined her head. Again Christina felt an understanding between them.

She knew what she was going to find.

She pulled back the cardboard. It was packed with soft white tissue paper. Wrapped inside was a little girl of glass.

Christina remembered the ghostly shape in the sketch, the outline of someone small. Now she saw long fair hair, round blue eyes, a blue dress and a sheaf of white lilies. The edge of the glass was ragged and splintered where it had been cut from the surroundings.

Christina turned to find Great Aunt May's eyes still on her. She knew May was well enough now to break the mystery. She ran over and took May's hands, stroking the tracery of scars.

'Floriane was the child stealer, wasn't she?'

Great Aunt May nodded.

Christina scrabbled in the suitcase for the paper and pencil.

'She stole my sister,' wrote May in tremulous letters.

'Did your parents get her back?' Christina was terrified of the answer.

After an age May wrote 'Yes.'

'Listen, Great Aunt May, I found some glass birds in that house. I knew the woman was there too. I took the birds back to the museum, to the woman in the window. She grew! She was all around us! She tried to enchant Grace, but I wouldn't let her. I gave her back her birds.' Christina's dreams were slowly piecing themselves together in her head. She said, 'In the end all she wanted was her glass birds, not real people at all. I suppose the glass birds can't escape from her like people could.'

Suddenly from her blurred dream Christina understood what May had done, years ago. She saw May, grown-up now, advancing towards the tall glass woman, with something held high above her head. She heard wails of rage echo round the room, saw the emerald eyes burn as May cut her glass sister free from the window. She said, 'How brave you were, Aunt May.'

Great Aunt May's hand shot out and grabbed Christina's wrist so hard it hurt. She hissed, 'Now she will rest at last!'

'You can speak!' cried Christina.

'Goodness me. So I can!' said the old lady, blinking with shock.

Christina knelt down by her and took her hand.

May said, 'You have broken the spell, dear. Because you stood up to her. She's got her birds back, but she's not having my sister. *Or* yours!' She turned to Christina with a wistful smile. 'I loved my little sister,' she said.

And I love Grace, thought Christina, *even*

though she's such a pest.

She said, 'Tell me the story of the window.'

Great Aunt May began, haltingly. 'When it happened, I was thirteen. My sister was six. Floriane came secretly to our home. I eavesdropped . . . she promised my sister presents if she went to the dark red house with her. I followed them,' May put her finger to her lips, 'because I felt envious.'

'Then what happened?'

'I climbed over those horrible iron gates. Hurt my hands. I knew something was wrong. I peeped through the big window and I saw my sister weeping.' Christina remembered the little girl in the dream, seeing a shadow behind the glass.

Great Aunt May whispered, 'Sometimes children know wickedness sooner than grown-ups do. Floriane wanted my father for herself. But he loved my mother.

Floriane was jealous, jealous as a serpent.'

'So what did you do?'

'I hurried all the way home. Got into terrible trouble for running away. They shut me in my room to punish me. I shouted and banged on the door for hours. In the end, when my sister didn't return home, they listened to me.'

'What happened to her?'

'My father rescued her. But she was fearful all her life. Floriane had sketched her for the window and so she believed she was under Floriane's spell. Her health was never very good. She died of tuberculosis. Yet I felt she still wasn't free of Floriane, not while she was in the window.'

Everything was clear now, except the very end. Christina had to know.

'What became of Floriane?'

'She fled abroad to Italy,' said Great Aunt

May. 'She died there. She was commissioned to make a big window for a castle. She cut a great eagle, out of golden glass. You remember how Floriane loved birds?'

'Yes,' said Christina, thinking of the pretty, captive swallows.

'Well my dear . . . Somehow the gold eagle fell from the window down onto Floriane. They say it cut her in two.'

'You didn't tell me Great Aunt May had a sister, Dad,' said Christina as they drove home. 'What was their name? I mean, their family name?'

'Oh, I think it was Dunne. Their father was an artist. Orlando, or some weird name. Funny lot, artists.'

'Funny Christina too,' murmured Grace, nestling up to her.

'I remember my uncle saying Great Aunt

May was devoted to her little sister,' said Dad.

'Like Christina. Christina looks after me,' said Grace. 'She keeps me safe.' She turned wide eyes up to Christina. 'Don't you,

Chrissie?'

Christina sighed. 'I suppose so,' she said. She felt in her pocket for a packet of mints. She hesitated, and then gave them to Grace. *In the nursing home Great Aunt May sleeps*

soundly in her chair, because the spell is broken at last.

Grace and Christina travel in their parents' car safely past the dark red house.

In the vast room there lie shards of glass, a spill of jewels on the stone floor. The February wind blows cold through the gaping window. The glass shimmers and shifts in memory.

In the museum the attendant begins the front page of his newspaper again.

Up on the wall behind him the woman of glass stands tall, her beloved birds trapped with her forever. Now her lips turn up in a smile.

You may think her green eyes have lost their glitter of ill-will.

If you wait awhile, you may see . . .

But you won't wait. Will you?

If you enjoyed
GHOST IN THE GLASS
look out for these other fantastic books!

The Boy Who Swallowed a Ghost
by Vivien Alcock

If the school champion turned to you
for help, would you refuse?

Mike is out of his depth. Prince – everyone's
hero – is terrified about something,
and he's turned to Mike for help.
Prince's story is too incredible to be true,
yet his fear is real enough, and this is
Mike's chance to save his idol.

But how can Mike help if he
doesn't even believe?

Dolphin Boy
by Julie Bertagna

Dibs can copy any sound – a police siren,
a helicopter, a car. Yet he can't communicate, except
through his drawings.

Only his sister, Amy, really understands him,
but even she wishes Dibs could be like
an ordinary brother.

Can a lost dolphin on the beach
help Dibs learn to speak?

SCOTTISH MAMMOTH

Doodlebug Alley
by Robert Swindells

It's World War II, and doodlebugs,
the deadliest bombs yet, are raining down on
London. No one is safe, no street intact.

The war is tearing Sandy's family apart.

Do they stand a chance in Doodlebug Alley?